Contents

Chapter 1

She was Priyanka Singh, young lass of 21 years having married a week ago to Parminder Singh, was on a trip to her mother's house, accompanied by her brother-in-law Raj who was 23 years of age.

Priyanka had taken this trip on the advice of her husband Parminder , who earlier having spoken to her mother Shilpa had sent with her a sealed envelope addressed to her. Priyanka was delighted to go to her mother's house and after traveling for 24 hours they reached the farm house situated some distance away from the nearest village.

Priyanka was born and bred in this farm house and as it was on the outskirts of the village she did not have any friends except the few children of their housekeepers and gardeners. As she was the only child of Ranjit and Shilpa she was pampered a lot and when Ranjit met with a fatal accident six months ago, his wife Shilpa saw that Priyanka was married off.

Shilpa had found in Parminder , a well established business man, most suitable partner for Priyanka and soon she had celebrated their wedding with pomp and gaiety.

This day Shilpa waited for her daughter and her brother-in-law Raj eagerly. She wanted to go through the letter which her son-in-law had talked about on the phone. She was a bit nervous and when she saw Priyanka she was relieved.

Raj was also happy to have accompanied his sister-in-law to this remote farm house. Earlier as they were traveling in a crowded train he has sat nudged to his sister-in-law and this nearness had sent warm sensations down his body. He looked forward for such close encounters.

Late in the evening as Priyanka handed over the sealed envelope to her, Shilpa on going through it both cried and laughed. She cried for not having spoken to her daughter about sex and smiled because it was going to be a new experience teaching her.

After she read the letter, Shilpa approached her daughter and casually asked "how is Parminder "

Priyanka went red in the face hearing his name and said "he is a rogue"

"Why do say so" asked her mother.

"Because he is a shameless creature and he has no manners" shot back an angry Priyanka.

"Why, what happened" asked her mother.

"He acts like a rogue during nights" replied Priyanka.

"And in the day" asked her mother.

"In the day he behaves normally" replied Priyanka.

"What does he do at nights that you are so angry with him" asked her mother.

"He has no shame and his acts are embarrassing" replied Priyanka.

"What does he do that is so embarrassing" asked her mother?

"I can't tell you what he does" saying this Priyanka walked away from her mother.

Shilpa smiled at her reply and when she looked up she saw Raj approaching.

Raj was a sturdy young guy very much like his brother. Seeing him coming down, Shilpa felt as if she was seeing Parminder striding down the stairs. He resembled him so much.

As the three sat and had their supper, Raj excused and went to this allotted room upstairs while both Priyanka and her mother sat back chatting.

When fifteen minutes passed since Raj had gone to his room, Shilpa looked at Priyanka and said "why don't you go up and see if he needs anything"

Hearing this Priyanka immediately got up and fetching a glass of milk took it up to his room.

Shilpa was glad to see her daughter take interest in her duties.

Priyanka in her eagerness to hand Raj milk entered the room without knocking. At first she did not see anything but when her eyes got accustomed to the room she saw Raj pulling his pajamas up standing at far corner. Priyanka was shocked to see her brother-in-law dressing up. She waited till he pulled his pajama up and tied the cord.

Coming forward and accepting the glass of milk Raj looked at his sister-in-law with want in his eyes which she could not muster. His eyes wandered over her body and when they devoured her figure he drew his eyes back to her face and said "how kind of you"

To his Priyanka smiled and asked "do you need anything"

"Yes, something to keep my body warm" he replied looking at her body.

"I will get a rug for you" saying it Priyanka turned and went out of the room.

Raj lying on the cot waited for her and when she entered without knocking, he had to adjust his erectness in his pajamas quickly.

Priyanka did not notice it and casually spread the blanket over Raj's body and tucking it over said "do you need anything else"

Raj was pleased to have Priyanka tuck the blanket under him and overwhelmed by her action he smiled at her said "so nice of you, no thanks."

To this Priyanka blushed and said "call me if you need anything"

"I need a cup of hot coffee in the morning" saying this he wished her goodnight.

Wishing him goodnight Priyanka went out of the room. Once inside her own room her thoughts drifted to her husband wondering what he would have done if he was present here. On the other hand seeing her brother-in-law who was so polite made her heart warm up to him. As she felt drowsy the last scene which came into her mind was Raj pulling his pajamas up over his bare legs. This vision haunted her and as she could not sleep she went to her mother's room.

Shilpa was awake when she heard Priyanka come in and lay beside her. The mother in her suddenly felt that she was disturbed and to soothe her she pulled her close. Priyanka on lying close to her mother felt relieved and soon sleep took over her.

The next morning Shilpa was surprised when she saw her daughter get up early and run to the kitchen. When she followed her she was pleased to see her brewing coffee and as she watched, Priyanka filling up one cup carried it upstairs. Shilpa watched her and felt relieved.

Carrying the cup of coffee Priyanka entered Raj's room without knocking. This time she saw him sleeping his body fully covered with the blanket. Keeping the cup at the table she moved closer to him and shook him awake.

Raj who was still dreaming of her was overjoyed to see his sister-in-law waking him up. Her hair was messed and her dress shriveled. When Priyanka presented him the cup of coffee she could not hold the sari which was slipping from her bosom.

Raj was rewarded by the sight of her heaving bosom. Priyanka followed his stare and could not understand what had attracted him. When Raj finally took the cup of coffee, Priyanka without straightening her sari went down stairs to find her mother eyeing up at her exposed bosom.

As she approached she heard her mother say "why don't you set your sari straight"

'Why? What's wrong in it" asked Priyanka looking down at the sari which had slipped from her bosom.

"You had been to Raj's room, you ought to have set it straight" she replied.

"I don't understand the need for it" saying this she went into her mother's bathroom. Standing before the full length mirror and seeing her reflection she was surprised. She saw how shriveled her dress was and how prominently her breasts were seen behind her blouse. Seeing herself in this state she instinctively covered her bosom and as her hands brushed her breasts a warm sensation crept through her body. She stood still enjoying the sensations and when she saw the figure of her mother looking up at her she blushed.

It was here that an idea germinated in Shilpa's mind and leaving her daughter alone as she came out of the room she thought of it. The more she thought of it the more she liked it. Feeling relieved she went in to take care of the breakfast.

Raj having finished his bath came down to the dining table and saw Priyanka blush when she looked at him. Wearing an ordinary sari, her wet hair bundled in a towel, tiny drops of water plastered on her face, she looked very pretty. As Raj was watching her he saw her mother step into the room carrying his breakfast. This made him shift his glance and when all sat down, he did not get any time to look up at Priyanka.

It was 10 am when Raj saw Priyanka dressed up in a rich sari go out with her maid and when he enquired with her mother where she had gone, he was surprised to hear that she had gone to learn cooking from a relative as desired by her husband. This upset him a little as she was expected to return back only in the evening.

Shilpa saw the change in him and to cheer him up she said "don't worry I have planned an outing for you"

When Raj heard this, his face brightened and it also made him take a closer look at Priyanka's mother. What he saw of her got imprinted in his mind. Shilpa was a woman who looked much younger than the age of 42. She was tall, well built and robust. Her features though on the heavier side were very attractive to the eyes. She possessed a rounded never die smiling face. Her chest was broad and her waist and hips were proportionate to it. On the whole she was a healthy attractive sensual woman.

Raj thoughts wandered on to the wrong side. He instinctively thought of possessing her. His mind went racing. Seeing him looking down at her Shilpa asked him to get ready to go out.

Hearing this Raj went to his room and putting on his jeans and a shirt he hurried back to see Shilpa sitting on the driver's seat of a small truck. As the vehicle was a left hand drive Raj sitting at her right had a clear view of her waistline which was exposed whenever she used her right hand to shift gears.

Shilpa drove the vehicle with ease all the time feeling Raj's stare at the exposed part of her body. His stare sent warm vibrations up her spine and she enjoyed his deep stares without letting him know she was flaunting him.

Soon they reached a vast stretch of vine yard and as they moved deep into it, they stopped near a big banyan tree. Getting down they strolled down the vineyard. Raj was more interested to be in her company than hearing her speak about the vine yard. Soon they came to a sprawling lake which had crystal clear water.

Pointing to the lake Shilpa laughed and said "this is our swimming pool"

"Do you swim" asked Raj enthusiastically.
"I used to but since I stopped you can see how I have blown up" she said.

"You are exaggerating. You are not so chubby" replied Raj.

"Ah! Thanks, that's very pleasing to hear" she replied.

"Does Priyanka swim" asked Raj?

"No she does not. She is scared of water" replied back Shilpa.

"I wish I had someone for company" said Raj looking at the lake.

"Let me see if I can join you some day" replied Shilpa hesitatingly.

"Oh! That would be pretty nice. I will be staying here only for a week and hope you would make up your mind soon" he said.

"Are you leaving so soon" she asked puzzled.

"Yes my flight is booked and I have to attend my final semester" he replied.

"Will you return after completing your studies" she asked and waited for his response.

"I have been selected and I think I will work for sometime before I return back" he replied.

"Oh! I wish you would come as soon as you completed your course" said Shilpa blushingly.

To this Raj smiled back at her and asked "do you want me to."

"Well, your brother will be glad to have some help in his business" she replied.

"He has to wait for a few years" saying it he strolled towards the lake and taking hold of some water he sprayed it over her.

Shilpa smiled at him as she wiped the droplets from her face lifting one end of her sari.

As Shilpa lifted her sari Raj had a glimpse of her bare waist up to her bosom which made him tremble. His attention was focused on her plump waist and Shilpa seeing him eying gave him enough time to ogle before covering herself.

To change the subject Shilpa said "I wish Priyanka was here"

"Yes, it would have been nice" replied Raj thinking of Priyanka.

"You two youngsters would have had some fun" replied Shilpa looking at the lake.

"But she does not swim" replied Raj.

"Yes, she does not swim but loves wading in knee deep water" replied Shilpa.

"I am hoping that you would join me" replied Raj shyly.

"I won't promise you but I will try" said Shilpa.

"Now" asked Raj?

"No, not today, I have not brought any towels" she replied.

"Then next time" saying this Raj went near the trunk of the banyan tree and sat down stretching his legs while Shilpa pulled out a basket from the truck.

As they both had light snacks and coffee Shilpa again shifted the topic to her daughter and said "I wonder what Priyanka is doing."

"You should know better as you have sent her" replied Raj.

"I had to as I had orders from her husband" said Shilpa.

"How many days more has she to attend" asked Raj?

"May be three to four days, then you both can visit this place" she said looking at him keenly searching for his reactions.

"Yes, meanwhile I would like to have your company" he replied.

Though his words pleased her, why can't he understand she thought out loudly?

'What" asked Raj hearing her murmur?

"I mean, you both being of the same age can have more fun" she replied.

"You are not that old" shot back Raj looking at her.

"You mean you don't mind being in my company" she asked? As she said this, she felt warmness creep up her body.

"Yes, I would rather be with you than wait for her" replied Raj.

"How sweet of you" saying this she stretched her legs on the smooth grass.

"I will be here only for a few days and I don't want to be left alone" said Raj.

"Okay my dear boy! I will be with you whenever Priyanka is out, happy" she asked.

Hearing this Raj was elated and sliding closer said "I am delighted"

"Why are you so interested to be in my company" asked Shilpa.

"Because you are very charming and I love your company" he replied.

"Are you talking to me or are you thinking of someone else" she asked.

"No, I mean it. I like your company more than that of any other chick" he replied.

"It's flattering and may I know what it is that attracts you to me" she asked.

"Why, you are charming, very pretty and it is an honor to be with you" he replied.

"Wow! You know very well how to please women" said Shilpa on hearing his words.

"I don't say it to every woman I meet" he replied.

"Then shall I consider myself to be lucky" she asked.

"You are blessed with such charms" answered back Raj.

"Oh! It is getting very personnel" she said smilingly and got up.

"Stay back" said Raj as he held her hand.

This took Shilpa by surprise and as she could not say no to him said "tomorrow we will stay back for a longer time, let's go now" she said.

"Fine" saying it Raj again held her hand for support and as she pulled him he got up. Soon they reached the farm house and both of them could not muster how time had flown when they were together.

As they went for a change they heard Priyanka's arrival. Her arrival depleted the charged atmosphere. Soon the conversation drifted back to what you did, what you learned, etc, etc, till it was time for Priyanka to go to Raj's room with a glass of milk.

Raj had timed Priyanka's arrival. He was in the process of removing his pants when Priyanka stepped into his room. Priyanka on seeing Raj drop his pants down did not move out of the room but bowed her head.

Raj exclaimed "Oh" as he heard Priyanka enter, then pulling on his pajamas and turning towards her he tied the cord. Priyanka from the corner of her eye saw the impression of his manhood and blushed at its sight.

Raj saw her steal a glance at his stance. This stimulated him and coming closer he held her hand which was holding the glass of milk.

Priyanka felt the warmth of his hand on hers. This intimacy heightened her senses. For the first time she liked the warm feelings and she let him fondle her hand for a couple of seconds before handing him the glass of milk.

"Don't you think it is very chill tonight" asked Raj.

"Yes" replied Priyanka moving towards the open windows.

Raj stood staring at her as she went on her heels to fix the latch of the windows. Her projected body looked sensuous from behind. He had the sudden desire to grasp her but he knew she was naïve. He felt he has to win her slowly. He closed the gap between the two and standing right behind her he held her waist to support her.

Priyanka again felt the warmness of his hands on her body. The chemistry of her body changed. The sensitive pores of her skin which were dead started to regain life. She let out a soft moan which died inside her mouth before reaching out.

Raj set her down slowly and when Priyanka turned to face him he said "now it is cozier."

"Yes, I have shut the windows" replied a smiling Priyanka.

"It is not because of that" said Raj.

"Then what" asked a confused Priyanka.

"It is because of your closeness" replied Raj.

"How does it help you" she asked, real concern showing on her face.

"The heat generated from your body keeps me warm" he replied.

"Is it" she asked perplexed by his answer.

"Yes, move closer, you will feel it too" he said.

Priyanka casually stepped closer to him and Raj placing his hands on her shoulders and squeezing them asked "do you feel it."

"Yes and I am amazed to feel the warmness without our bodies touching" replied Priyanka.

"It will be warmer when our bodies feel touch each others" Raj spoke softly.

"Yes it's true" answered Priyanka feeling warmer as she moved close to him.

"Get closer" said Raj sliding his hands from her shoulders on to her back.

Priyanka felt his hands slide down from her shoulders on to her back. This made her body grow warmer and she stood still visualizing how it would be if her body touched his. She shuddered at this thought and hesitatingly moved an inch further and asked "will this do."

"No, put your arms around my back and hug me" replied Raj getting excited by the very thought of it.

"This way" asked Priyanka as she put her arms around his neck and placed her face on his chest.

"Yes, that's it" said Raj as he tightened the hold upon her.

Priyanka's cheeks felt the warmth of his chest and when Raj tightened the hold she gripped his neck hard once before coming out of his hug.

Raj on seeing a blushing Priyanka asked "did you feel the warmth."

"Yes" replied Priyanka.

"It will be warmer if you hug me properly" he said.

To this Priyanka smiled and shaking her head moved towards the bed.

Raj knowing he had to bid his time went across the room and lay on the bed waiting for Priyanka to pull the blanket over him.

Priyanka took the blanket in her hand and spreading it over his feet she dragged it up to his chest.

Raj as he felt that Priyanka having completed her assignment was sure to walk out of the room held her hand and bringing to his mouth, kissed it lightly.

Priyanka's body shivered at the touch of his warm lips on her cool hand. She did not know what had possessed her body. Pulling her hand away from his mouth she turned and left the room.

This time she did not enter her mother's bedroom but went directly to her own room. There she recapped all that had taken place and when she recalled the scenes her body started to wriggle. Her senses had blossomed and she loved every bit of it. Every part of her body itched to be touched and touching it, she felt moistness between her thighs. Turning her face on the soft pillow and hugging it, she slept peacefully.

Next morning a totally different Priyanka was awake. As she looked up in the mirror to adjust her dress she saw her cheeks had turned crimson. They were red and glistening with the morning light. Putting the comb through her hair she rushed to the kitchen and brewing coffee took it up stairs.

Raj hearing her feeble feet outside his room quickly pulled his pajama up, exposing one leg up to his thighs feigned sleep. Priyanka on entering his room was presented with the sight of his exposed leg. She stood staring at it and when Raj turned; her gaze got shifted on the impression of his half erect manhood.

Chapter 2

Priyanka was in a dilemma standing over there looking at him. The position in which Raj lay exposed she could not go near him and shake him. She called out by his name once, twice and on the third count Raj opened his eyes to see a scintillating Priyanka standing in front of him. She looked different. She had changed. Her face was flushed, her eyes shinning, her cheeks red, her lips pouting. He felt enchanted to see her.

Pulling the blanket and covering up his bare leg he patted the empty space on the bed signaling her to sit. Priyanka sat at the edge of the bed and handed him the cup of coffee. Raj sitting up on the bed took the cup of coffee from her.

Taking a sip he looked at Priyanka who was blushing sitting close to him. Priyanka waited till he finished his coffee and when the cup was empty as she took it Raj held her hand.

This made Priyanka to look up at him. Raj smiled at her and holding her hand he started feeling her fingers. Priyanka let him fondle her fingers and before she could pull them, he took them to his mouth and kissed them.

Priyanka blushed again but this time she did not pull back her hand. This prompted Raj to slide her middle finger inside his mouth and suck it. Priyanka let out a soft moan which was audible. Raj continued sucking her fingers one by one and also slowly pulled Priyanka up on his chest.

On being pulled up, "are you feeling cold" asked Priyanka?

"Yes, it is very cold here and I need the warmth of your body" replied Raj.

"But I have to get ready to attend my class" said Priyanka.

"Stay back for a while" saying it Raj pulled up her and hugged her.

As Raj took her in his arms Priyanka felt her bosom smash against his chest. This sent a hot wave through her body. Her body sizzled with delight and instinctively she put her arms around his back and held him.

Raj gripped her more tightly and taking hold of her face in his hands he drew it up and looking into her eyes said "Priyanka you are very pretty."

Priyanka blushed and said "I have to go"

"Can you not stay for some time" asked Raj.

"It is getting late" replied Priyanka.

"I wish you could stay back for some time" said Raj.

"Why" asked Priyanka blushingly?

"Because it gives me pleasure to hold you like this" said Raj hugging Priyanka tightly.

"Then you have to wait" said Priyanka trying to get up.

"I can't wait" replied Raj drawing her face near to his.

"Cant wait for what" asked Priyanka.

"This" saying it he kissed Priyanka on her lips.

"Dhat" saying this Priyanka got up and ran out of his room blushingly.

Shilpa saw a blushing Priyanka come down the stairs and stand in front of her. Embracing her; "what happened" she asked softly?

"He kissed me" replied a bashful Priyanka.

"So what if he kissed" said her mother.

"You don't know where he kissed me" replied back Priyanka.

"Where did he kiss you" asked her mother hugging her daughter.

"He kissed me on my lips" she said softly.

Hearing it Shilpa was delighted. She was glad that the drama she had thought of enacting was done by Raj. Embracing Priyanka in her arms she said "it's okay, he is your brother-in-law."

"So what if he is my brother-in-law" asked a puzzled Priyanka.

"There is no harm in it and moreover I think he is feeling very lonely over here" said her mother.

Her mother's words made Priyanka to ponder for a while. Pulling up she said "Yes, I think he is getting bored up. Take care of him till I return" saying this she went to change.

Shilpa was delighted to hear her words. At one hand she felt relieved as her main problem was going to be solved and on the other "take care of him till I return" these words kept ringing in her ears.

After Priyanka left Shilpa went to her room to change. After lot of trails as she stepped out wearing a light blue color sari and a matching sleeveless blouse she was confronted by Raj who openly looked at her.

She blushed when the roving eyes of Raj went over her body. Trying to shake him up, "shall we go" she said.

"Yes, but don't forget to carry towels" replied Raj looking up at a blushing Shilpa.

Turning back to go to her room she said "you don't easily forget things."

"No, I don't" replied Raj loudly.

"And also you are very adamant" said Shilpa as she went inside.

Raj smiled at her words and waited to escort her to the truck.

Once settled in the cozy truck Raj was excited when he saw her wearing a sleeveless blouse. His eyes wandered over her bare arms and on one occasion as Shilpa pulled her right hand up his eyes were rewarded with the dark patch of hair under her armpits. This sight aroused him and Raj swiftly moved his eyes away from the spot.

Shilpa had been watching him in the rearview mirror. She had deliberately lifted her arm exposing her armpit and when Raj shifted his gaze from her, a smile appeared on her face.

Soon they reached the farm. This time Shilpa steered the truck through dense foliage and came on the other side of the lake. The place was secluded.

Shilpa was the first to alight from the truck and standing by the side of the truck she lifted both her hands up to tie her hair in a bun. Raj had a full view of her striking figure basking in the sun. He saw the curve of her hips, her bulky waistline, her robust breasts and the patch of silky black hair covering her armpits.

Shilpa smiled at Raj whose eyes were feasting upon her body and asked "is not the weather lovely today."

"Yes, it is good to be out in the sun after a chill night" replied Raj.

"Was it very chill at night" asked Shilpa still tying her hair.

"Yes, your place is very cold" replied Raj.

"Do you want a heater to be placed in your room" said Shilpa.

"Yes, that would keep my body warm" said Raj eyeing at her body and implicating it.

Shilpa blushed to what his words implied and said "come we will take a stroll"

To this Raj extended his hand and Shilpa held it in hers softly.

Holding each others hand they started walking and this closed the gap between the two. As they neared the lake Raj let his knuckle brush her thighs.

Shilpa felt his knuckles brace her thighs and she slid closer letting his knuckles feel more of her warm thighs.

This prompted Raj to move closer to her and when he opened his fingers to slide above her thighs Shilpa trudged on a stone and slipped. Raj immediately slid his hand on her waist and held her before she could fall.

Saying "thanks" Shilpa too put her hand on his waist for support.

Raj was delighted as Shilpa slid her hand on his waist. Pulling her closer he glued his hand over her upper thighs and feeling the warmth of her body he trudged along.

Shilpa too held him closer and when his hands were idle she let her body sway a little, letting her thighs brush his whenever they came across any hurdles. Both were conscious of each others bodies touching but kept their cool, content with the warmness generated from it.

They walked around in circles before they saw a huge boulder lying near the lake. Removing their footwear and wading through ankle deep water they sat side by side on it.

It was then that Raj without being noticed bent forward and taking some water sprinkled it on her face. Shilpa shivered at the sudden spurt of water on her face and to avoid more of it she hid her face on Raj's chest saying "no" halfheartedly.

As Shilpa hid her face on his chest, Raj placing his hand on her shoulders drew her closer to him and with the other he lifted some more water and started spraying it over her face.

"Stop it Raj" protested Shilpa meekly.

Hearing her half hearted protests Raj lifted her up slightly and aiming at her neck sprinkled on it.

"What are you doing" said Shilpa smilingly as she held the top of her sari and started wiping the droplets from her face and neck.

As Shilpa lifted the sari to wipe her face, her chest was exposed and Raj eyes took to her heaving bosom. His stare was so intense that Shilpa feeling the warmness engulfing her body quickly brought back the sari down and covering her bosom said "enough of looking my dear boy"

Hearing her bold statement Raj held the top of her sari and trying to push it aside said "let me"

"No you are not supposed to" replied back Shilpa laughingly as she covered her chest.

"Why" asked Raj continuing to pull her sari.

"Because I don't think you are entitled to" she said tightening her hold on the sari.

Seeing her grip the sari and not allowing him, Raj held her face in his hands and said "when will I be entitled to see."

"Maybe when you grow up a little" she said bringing her face down and brushing his nose with hers.

"Then can I ask for something else" he asked caressing her cheeks with his hands.

"And what is that" she asked laughingly as his fingers reached her lips.

"This" he said bracing her lips with his fingers sensually.

"And what is that for" she asked teasingly.

"I want to. . . . . . . touch them" he said as he could not say "kiss them"

"You are touching them" she replied hoisting her face over his lips.

"No I mean this" he said as he brought out his tongue and moistened his lips.

"Yes, what is it that you want" she said brushing his cheeks with her lips.

"I want to kiss you" he said getting excited by her closeness.

"Kiss me, like you kissed Priyanka" she asked.

"Yes, how do you know about it" he said softly.

"Nothing is hidden from me" she replied nuzzling her face on his cheeks.

"Yes, I want to kiss you like I kissed Priyanka" he replied.

"On my lips" she asked bringing her lips close to his.

"Yes, on your lips" saying this he placed his lips on hers.

As soon as Raj's lips contacted hers Shilpa's body shivered with excitement and holding him tightly she smacked her lips on his and kissed him back.

Raj let out a deep moan on being kissed, he was aroused and before he could embrace her, Shilpa was out of his reach and as he looked for her he saw her wading in the ankle deep water.
Shilpa after having kissed him was aroused. She had come out of his arms as she was scared of the things that would have followed. Wading through the water she was contemplating what to do next. Though her body craved for sex, her mind was deeply troubled. At one hand her body desired for it and on the other she was worried as to what her daughter would say about it.

As these thoughts ran in her mind she consoled her self by the fact, what she was doing was for her daughter's sake. The welfare of her daughter was utmost in her mind. This thought gave her some respite and recouping her mind she strolled lazily towards the parked truck.

Raj watched keenly as Shilpa took a leisure walk. The view of her undulating posterior aroused him and the front of his pants was swollen signifying the state of his manhood. To hide it from her he quickly removed his shirt and Jeans and dived into the water.

Shilpa heard the sound of water splashing and as she turned she saw Raj swimming. She stood looking at him swim with ease and when he turned to return back, she picked up the towel and met him as he came out of water.

Raj after taking the towel from her tried to grasp her but Shilpa eluded him. Drying himself and tying the towel on his waist he slid beside Shilpa, who after having laid out the snacks was resting on her back on the trunk of a tree.

Sitting close to her Raj was drawn by the fragrance from her body. He dipped his head on her shoulders and inhaling the aroma said "you smell beautiful"

Shilpa smiled at him and to change the topic asked "did you enjoy the swim."

"Yes, but I wish I had your company" he replied nuzzling his wet head on her shoulders.

"I will join sometime, meanwhile take this towel and dry your hair, it is wet" she replied.

"No, let me use your sari" saying this he drew the top of her sari and started brushing it over his wet hair.

"Hey, you are dampening my sari" she replied.

"Yes I know and I want to use it" he replied.

"May I know why it is so" she asked her eyes quizzing him.

"Because it is soft and moreover it smells beautiful" he replied inhaling its fragrance and drawing much of her sari out.

Shilpa seeing her sari being pulled away from her bosom held to some part of it and said "hey, you are pulling it out"

"So what" asked Raj?

"I feel exposed" she replied softly.

"Your body is well covered. Imagine how it would appear if you are in swimsuit" he said.

"Yes, that is the reason why I have not joined you for a swim" she replied.

"It is not fair, be sportive" he said.

"I can't" she replied shyly.

"Why cant you" he persisted.

"I have put up much weight and it would be embarrassing" she replied.

"You would look swell in it. You have a great figure" he said as he pushed aside her sari and stared at her bosom.

"Do you think so" she asked seeing him looking at her bosom.

"Yes, a two piece suit would look fabulous on you" he said as he stared at her waistline and voluptuous hips.

"I thought my hips are too large" she replied.

"No these are perfect for your age" he said as he slid his hand on her thighs and moved it up her hips.

"Well if you think it is okay, then fine" she said.

Hearing it Raj was thrilled and suddenly he kissed her on the cheeks.

"What was that for" she asked when he kissed her on the cheeks.

"It was for having agreed for the swim" he replied.

"Why are getting crazy thinking of me joining you for a swim" she asked.

Raj could not immediately answer her back. He thought for a second and said "it would be great to have your company in the water."

"Even now I can join you, what's the difference" she asked getting excited by his reply.

Moving his lips closer to his ears he replied "your clothing makes a lot of difference" he replied.

"You mean you want me to join you wearing a swim suit" she asked lightly?

"Yes, I would love to see you in a swim suit" saying this he pecked his lips on hers.

"I see. Isn't it a fact that my dear boy wants me to wear a swim suit so that he can ogle at me" saying this she kissed him back on his lips.

"Yes, I want to see your beautiful body draped in a swim suit" he replied, squarely placing his lips on hers and kissing her hard.

"You are a lucky boy" she said removing her lips from his.

"Why is it so" asked Raj.

'For having kissed two women today" she replied softly.

"Oh! That was nothing compared to this" he said trying to kiss her again.

Pushing his face away from hers, "did you not like kissing Priyanka" she asked?

"No, Priyanka is inexperienced and kissing her did not excite me much as this" he lied.

"Why don't you teach her then" she shot out impulsively.

"I will if you want me to" he said and looked into her eyes.

"She needs a few lessons" she replied shyly.

"I am of the same opinion" he said as he placed his hand again on her thighs.

"You are right; she needs some assistance" muttering these words to herself, she said "shall we go now" when she felt his hand start to caress her thighs.

"Can we not stay back for a while, it is cozy here" whispered Raj feeling the warmth of her thighs.

"Priyanka might have come home" said Shilpa brushing her lips on his cheeks.

"Oh! I did not know it was so late" he replied as he brought his face down.

"Time flies fast my dear boy" she replied holding his head and nuzzling his face on her neck.

Knowing pretty well it was time to go, Raj planting a kiss on the nape of her neck got up.

Shilpa tidying up her dress got up and took up the job of driving. Both were silent on way back home. Both were thinking of the things to come and when they reached home they saw that Priyanka had not reached yet.

Raj taking the initiative held Shilpa's hand. Shilpa was surprised at this and when she turned to question him he took her in his arms.

"Priyanka might come" said Shilpa as he hugged her.

"One kiss" muttered Raj releasing his hold on her.

"My dear boy, you are crazy" saying this Shilpa placed her hands on his shoulders and drawing his face near, kissed him passionately.

Raj was aroused by the kiss and before Shilpa could walk away he kissed her hard on her lips and slid his hand on her buttocks.

"You are getting impatient" saying this Shilpa went to her room.

Soon Priyanka came home and everyone remained silent.

After dinner Raj went up to his room. Priyanka sat chatting with her mother and when she did not get up mother said "why don't you give him some milk."

"Shall I" asked Priyanka as if she wanted her permission to do so.

"Yes, you better go before he sleeps" replied Shilpa.

Priyanka was glad that she had her mother's permission. As she climbed the stairs she felt warm sensations creep up her body. Hesitating a little she casually entered his room.

Raj was lying on the bed without his shirt on. He had placed his hands under his head exposing his bare chest and hairy armpits. On entering, Priyanka had a look at his hairy chest and underarms which was very striking to look at. Moving inside she said "are you not feeling cold today"

"No, your mother has fixed a room heater" he replied.

"Then you may be feeling cozy" she said handing him the glass of milk.

"Well the room is cozy but I need something warm" he replied indicating her to sit beside him.

"I know what makes you feel warm" saying this, she sat on the bed beside him handing him the hot milk.

"So kind of you" saying this he took the glass of milk and drank it in one go.

"Why are you in such a hurry" asked Priyanka taking the empty glass from him and setting it aside.

"Because you have the tendency to run away" he replied entangling his fingers in the locks of her hair.

"I went because I had to attend my cooking classes" she replied.

"Will you stay back for sometime now" he asked pulling her head down on his chest.

"I just came to give you milk" she replied smilingly as she settled her face on his bare chest.

"You know you are too naïve" he replied fondling the thick strands of her hair, pushing them aside and exposing her back.

As Priyanka felt his hand on her back she cuddled her face on his chest.

Seeing her placed uncomfortable, "why don't you stretch your feet" said Raj.

Hearing it Priyanka stretched herself on the bed beside him.

Raj was elated by this. His hand which was on her back started to draw circles on her back, circling her shoulders and waist softly.

This stimulated Priyanka and she started to take deep breaths.

Seeing her getting enthused Raj started massaging her shoulder blades lightly and when she let out a soft moan he slid his hands under her armpits and lifted her up.

On being pulled Priyanka hid her face on his shoulders.

Raj did not force things. He let her calm down and giving her few moments of respite he held her face in his hands and drawing it up said "you are very beautiful"

Priyanka blushed at his words and closed her eyes.

"Your cheeks are so rosy" saying this he planted a soft kiss on her cheeks.

As Raj kissed her cheeks Priyanka opened his eyes. She looked deep into his face. Her eyes took to his radiant eyes, his youthful face, and his hard lips and fell in love with it.

Raj smiled at her and lifting a finger brushed her soft lips and said "your lips are so promiscuous"

Hearing it she blushed again and said "you are very bad Raj"

"Why do you think I am bad" asked Raj as he encircled his hands on her back and drew her close.

"Because you kissed me on my lips" replied Priyanka.

"Should I not kiss your lips" asked Raj softly.

"You are not supposed to kiss your sister-in-law" replied Priyanka shyly.

"Then can my sister-in-law kiss me" he asked in reply.

Chapter 3

"**I**s it not the same thing" she asked him while her eyes were gleaming with passion.

"Yes it is the same thing. What shall I do, they are so mesmerizing" he said as he caressed her lips with his fingers.

These words ignited the passion inside her body. She opened her mouth slowly and when Raj slid his finger inside her mouth her body squirmed with pleasure and she said "It feels good."

"You will like this even more" saying this he pulled her down and kissed her lips softly.

"Oh! Raj" moaned Priyanka.

Embracing her tightly in his arms Raj kissed her lips passionately.

Priyanka's body trembled with desire and on impulse she kissed him back.

Raj tightening his hold on her ravaged her lips with his and when Priyanka reciprocated his kisses he pushed his tongue inside her mouth.

Priyanka opened her mouth wide allowing his tongue to penetrate deep inside her mouth and subconsciously put her arms around his back and held him.

This was what Raj was waiting for and the moment she held him, Raj curling her body upon his slid his hand between their bodies and placed his hand on her blouse feeling the soft contours of her breasts.

Priyanka was exhilarated. Her body shook with spasms and loving every bit of it she lifted herself a little allowing Raj's hand easy access to her breasts.

Raj brought the other hand down and caressing the upper part of her breasts he started to unhook her blouse.

Priyanka's body was on fire. The raw sensations creeping over body compelled her to kiss him back passionately and when Raj got through unhooking the top hooks of her blouse she slid her tongue inside his mouth and locked her lips on his mouth.

This heightened their pleasure and Raj after unhooking all the hooks pushed his hand inside her blouse and cupped her breasts over her bra.

This was the ultimate move that Priyanka could withstand and the moment his hand cupped her breasts Priyanka let out a deep moan and climaxed.

Raj felt her body tremble. He knew she had discharged and to heighten her pleasure he groped both her breasts in his hands and caressed them. Priyanka's body convulsed and after a few moments when she regained her self-control she opened her eyes to see the beaming face of Raj.

"Liked it" asked Raj removing his hands from her breasts and holding her face.

Priyanka dipped her face down in response and uttered "yes"

"This is what happens when two people kiss and fondle each other" said Raj embracing her in his arms.

"Did you like it too" asked Priyanka lifting her face.

"I was more interested in pleasing you" said Raj kissing her lips again.

"I think I better go now" said Priyanka.

"No wait for a while" saying this Raj flipped her on the bed and moved his body over hers.

Priyanka was again aroused as she felt his body crush hers. This time she pulled his face down and kissed him hard.

Raj was ecstatic. He put his arms around her back and drawing her slim body underneath his he pressed his fuming cock on her waist.

Priyanka felt the heat generated from his lions on her waist. She again squirmed in delight and holding his body onto hers she hugged him.

Raj went wild with desire. He started pushing his cock on her waist and as Priyanka squirmed he set aside her sari and blouse and bringing his hands down on her breasts he squeezed them in his hands.

Priyanka let out a load moan. She started calling out his name passionately. This infused Raj and he started pounding his cock on her warm soft waist. He was on the verge of shooting his cum.

Priyanka instinctively pushed her hands down and placing them just above his buttocks she held them tightly as the second round of discharge took over her body.

Raj slipped his hands inside her bra and feeling the warm flesh of her soft breasts he shot his cum screaming her name.

Meanwhile Priyanka too had felt her dam bursting for the second time. This was pure joy which she had never anticipated and when Raj slid on to her side after ejaculating she was abashed at seeing her blouse open and the straps of her bra slid aside revealing the top of her breasts.

Immediately pulling over her sari she got up and scampered out of his room. This time she went directly to her mother's room and seeing her mother awake she slid on her bed and lying by her side she hugged her.

Shilpa was surprised to see Priyanka come into her room and cuddle close to her. Making room for her she hugged her daughter. Priyanka feeling the warmness of her mother's body snuggled her face on her bosom.

Shilpa at once pulled her daughters face on her bosom and when Priyanka burrowed her face deeper onto her bosom, instinctively she started unhooking her own blouse.

Priyanka felt her mother unhooking her blouse. She lifted her face till her mother could draw out her blouse and once it was out she dipped her face on the warm buxom on her mother and embraced her.

Shilpa felt her daughter's soft lips and cheeks caressing her bosom. This invigorated her and before Priyanka could stop doing so, she slipped her hand over her daughter's chest and was surprised to see her blouse being unhooked. This heightened her desire. Pulling out her daughter's blouse from her body she held her in her arms.

Priyanka was aroused. She did not know what had taken over her body. She felt as if she was possessed as her hands slid behind her mother's back and unlatched her bra and once her mother's breasts were bare she put her mouth on her nipples and started sucking them.

This heightened her mother's pleasure and Shilpa instinctively unhooked her daughter's bra and when her breasts were left bare she caressed them while her daughter continued sucking her nipples.

Feeling her daughter's soft warm breasts Shilpa's body was on fire. Giving room to her daughter she pushed her breast into her mouth and as Priyanka sucked it, Shilpa slipped her hand from her daughter's breasts down and started caressing the warm flesh of her waist.

Priyanka felt her mother's hand on her bare waist. This made her to suck her nipples harder and Shilpa enjoying her nipples being sucked pushed her hand down till she felt her daughter's moist cunt over her dress.

This made Priyanka to scream out in pleasure. Saying, "touch me, touch me" she lifted her mouth from her mother's breasts and kissed her mother hard on her lips.

Shilpa was ecstatic by her daughter's kiss. Lifting her daughter's body over hers she slipped her hand inside her dress and fondled her wet sex over her panties.

Priyanka screamed again and let out her juices for the third time that night. Her body started to thrash upon her mother's and Shilpa feeling the pounding of her daughter's body over hers, engaged herself in kissing her daughter passionately and when her desires shot up, slipping her hot tongue inside her mouth she too climaxed.

Her discharge was so intense that it took her a couple of minutes before she could breathe easily. Both women were famished and as Priyanka slid down from her body, Shilpa covered her with a blanket and both slept peacefully.

Chapter 4

It was late in the morning when Shilpa was awake. Seeing her daughter fast asleep she got up and after tidying herself up she went into the kitchen to brew the coffee.

It was her turn to take coffee up to Raj's room. Raj who had anticipated Priyanka was pleasantly surprised to see Shilpa. He was lying on the bed with only his shorts on and on seeing Shilpa enter the room he was immediately aroused.

Shilpa took a fleeting glance of him before he pulled a sheet to cover his body and when she held the cup of coffee to him he slipped his hand on her waist.

Shilpa was surprised by this move. She stared at him and looked at the door indicating Priyanka was at home.

Raj without removing his hand from her waist drank the coffee and after placing the cup on the table he pulled her close.

Shaking her head Shilpa timidly sat on the bed and when she felt Raj's hand creeping up her from her waist towards her bosom she looked into his eyes questioning his actions. "It is so warm and so nice" he said feeling the soft flesh of her waistline.

"I know it is warm, you better behave" replied back a grinning Shilpa.

"Come closer" said Raj pulling her.

"What for" asked a shy Shilpa moving closer.

"For a kiss to start the day with" he replied.

"Do you always start the day with a kiss" she asked shaking her hair from her face and poking her nose on his.

"It is only here that my day starts with a kiss" he replied brushing his lips over her cheeks.

"And what do you do when you are at home" she asked laughingly.

"I dream about it" he replied planting wet kisses on her cheeks.

"Whom do you fantasy in your dreams" she asked getting stimulated by his hot tongue lapping her cheeks.

"A gorgeous woman like you" he said as his tongue searched for her lips.

"And what do you do to her" she asked sticking out her tongue and brushing it on his cheeks.

"I take her in my arms and kiss her," as he said as he pressed his lips on hers and kissed her hard.

"You are a little rogue this morning" saying this she got up.

"It is your presence which makes me one" he replied contend with having kissed her.

"Is it my presence or is it the same with other woman" she asked thinking about Priyanka.

"You are topmost in my thoughts" he replied.

"And then comes Priyanka is it" she asked?

"Yes everyone else is secondary" he said as he tried again to catch her.

"Then I think I would better stay away from you" saying this she moved out of his reach.

"For how long" he shot back.

"That, only time will tell" she replied laughingly as she left the room.

It was then he felt sure that he had her and to what extend she may be oblige, as she had said; only time would tell. Thinking of it he got up merrily.

Shilpa was happy with the start of the day. As she finished her work and Priyanka left, she went into room and started rummaging her wardrobe. She was looking for skirt and a top which she had not worn since a long time. As she found she was thrilled as it was a long flowing skirt which was soft to the touch. Dousing some perfume on her body she put on her two piece swim suit underneath the top and the skirt.

Feeling lighthearted she stepped out of the house and found the wind blowing at her skirt stimulating. She hastened her steps towards the truck and pressed hard on the horn which only made Raj laugh who meanwhile was close by.

As Raj stepped inside the car he was pleased to see the way Shilpa was dressed. The tight top which she had worn was showing off her bosom and the long green skirt was striking to look at. He stood staring at her and could not stop himself from saying "you look gorgeous."

Shilpa blushed at his words and said "do you intend to step in or stand there all day gazing"

"I don't mind standing all day looking at you" replied back Raj.

"Well if that is case, shall I put back the truck in the garage" asked Shilpa smilingly.

"You can do that after we return" saying this he jumped into the truck.

"It is very difficult to manage boys of your age" she said when Raj sat by her side.

"And it is equally difficult to be with a gorgeous woman like you" replied back Raj.

"Oh! You are too much and I can't win over you" shot back Shilpa.

"You can always win me with your charms" he replied back.

This made Shilpa to turn crimson and blushingly she said "shall we go now"

"Yes take me" he replied smilingly.

To this Shilpa stared at him and shaking her head and without replying back to him she started the truck.

All long the journey Raj was busy eying her body and inhaling the fragrance from it. It took some time to reach the farm as Shilpa was pre-occupied with the events that were to follow. As her thoughts wandered, a warm desire swept across her body.

When they reached the secluded spot and Shilpa stopped the truck, she was unable to move as she felt her feet were laden with lead. Raj jumping out of the truck went to her side and opening the door outstretched his hands.

Shilpa was overwhelmed by his action and sliding out of the truck she held his hand. Holding her hand Raj drew her out and sliding his own over her waist he drew her close to his body and started strolling down the graveled path.

Much to her surprise, Shilpa found Raj moving up towards the hillock instead of going down to the lake. Giving him the reins she enjoyed being with him and tamely followed him.

Soon they climbed the hillock and standing at the top Raj turned and facing her said "I am enchanted to be in your company"

"It's my pleasure too" she replied back moving closer.

"I don't know how to thank you" he said holding her face in his hand.

"You are my guest and it is my duty to accompany you" she replied placing her head on his shoulders.

"I cannot believe this is true" he said.

"Why can't you believe it" she asked.

"I couldn't have dreamt of it earlier" he said untying her hair and letting it fly loose.

"You are not dreaming this is real" she said cuddling closer to him.

"Yes and it is hard to accept the fact that I am here with a beautiful woman" he said.

His words were very encouraging and the more he talked about her the more she liked him and moving out of his arms she sat down on top of the hillock and motioned him to sit beside her.

Raj slid by her side and placing his hand on her thigh and feeling the soft material of her dress said "the skirt looks good on you"

"Oh! Thank you" replied Shilpa.

"And it is very fortunate too" he said.

"Why" asked Shilpa softly?

"Because it is on you" he replied.

"So what" she asked looking at him.

"It is lucky as it is touching and feeling your warm body" he said.

"Does it have feelings too" Shilpa asked getting excited by his talk.

"Yes and that is why it looks fabulous" he replied as he started caressing her thighs, pulling up her skirt.

"Where did you learn to use such words" she asked loving every moment.

"The presence of a gorgeous woman brings them out" he replied as he continued pulling her skirt up.

"Do you say the same to every women" she asked.

"No it is meant exclusive for you" he replied.

"Why don't you like other women" she said nibbling his ears.

"Other women don't possess such lovely legs" he said as he drew her skirt up and exposed her legs.

"So all these words are for my legs and not for me" she asked.

"It is for you as you own them" he said pulling her skirt further up.

"Is it because I own them or is it because I am letting you see them" she asked.

"You are letting me see them because they are lovely otherwise you would have hid them" he replied uncovering her legs up to her knees.

Unable to answer him back she said "can we go down now"

"I have much more to see" he replied pulling her skirt further up.

"You can see them when we go for a swim" she replied softly.

"This is more thrilling" he replied pulling her skirt up delicately.

"Why do you think so" she asked getting excited by his answers.

"A half dressed woman looks more sensuous than a naked one" he replied.

"I did not mean to go naked before you" she deftly put the words in his ears.

"I know that, but underneath it you are wearing your swim suit isn't it" he asked.

"How do you know that I am wearing my swim suit" she asked nibbling his ears.

"Because I did not see you carrying one when we got down from the truck" he replied.

"So what if I did not carry any" she asked.

"As you said you would not swim naked" he replied partially baring her thighs.

"So you keep track of all things" she asked as warmness crept over her body.

"Yes, and I can also say the color of the swim suit you are wearing" he replied looking at her waist.

"May I know which color it is" she asked getting thrilled by the fact.

"It is the color which suits your body the most" he replied looking at her well manicured thighs.

"And that is" she asked breathing harder.

"Obviously a black one and it is covering . . . . . ." he did not complete the sentence.

"Covering what" she let go of the words subconsciously.

"Covering your charms" he replied as he lifted her skirt up and looked at her thighs up to her swim suit.

Shilpa turned bluish on hearing his words and when he started to look down at her naked thighs she crisscrossed them hiding the most vulnerable spot from his gaze.

"That's not fair" said Raj as she crisscrossed her legs.

"Why do you think so" she asked.

"You had promised I can look up" he replied.

"You just saw it, isn't it" she asked.

"I want to see more" he said.

"Wait till we go for a swim" she replied.

"And why not now" he said placing his hand on her thighs.

"This is totally a different place and moreover it is getting too personal my dear boy" she said getting up.

"I don't see how different it is. Is it not the same legs and thighs which I am going to see later" he asked.
"Yes they are the same and you can see them when we swim, shall we go now" she said adamantly.

"Do we have to" he asked again.

"Yes, why" she asked.

"It was getting thrilling" he replied.

"I know it was getting thrilling my dear boy" saying this she pulled him up.

Getting up they trekked down the hillock and on reaching the lake Raj said "now what are you going to do."

"Meaning" she asked.

"Are you not joining me for a swim" he asked.

"Yes I am" she replied.

"With your skirt and top on" he asked.

"No I am going to remove them" she replied authoritatively.

"No you don't" he replied back moving close to her.

This shocked her and when she looked at him, "allow me to do so" he said.

"What" she screamed as a jolt of current passed through her body.

"I would love to have the pleasure of undressing you" he said while his eyes pleaded.

Shilpa could not decline his request. Turning her back to him she said "okay."

Raj was delighted when she accepted. Moving close to her he put his hands on her waist and clutching the seam of her top in both his hands he drew it over her body.

Shilpa stood shivering with excitement and when Raj pulled the top over her body she lifted her arms allowing him to remove it.

After pulling out the top Raj let his eyes wander over her curvaceous back. He felt ecstatic to see her broad shoulders, her well muscled back, her curved spine and coming down he was amazed to see the upper part of her buttocks protruding out of her skirt.

Getting excited he moved his hands on her waistline searching for the cord which held her skirt. Failing to reach it his hands wandered over her body and Shilpa feeling his hands on her body laughed at his predicament and said "just pull it down"

Hearing it Raj slid his fingers inside her skirt and holding the soft texture of her skirt he slid it down her silken body slowly, all the time his eyes gazing over the curves of her body.

Once the skirt slid from her body, Shilpa stepping out of it ran and dived into water before Raj could ogle at her figure leisurely.

Raj smiled as he saw her running and quickly removing his clothes he followed her in his brief shorts.

Shilpa being adept to the lake and a good swimmer she was a distance away from him. Raj moving at a fast pace quickly joined her. They swam in unison for some time and when he saw she was getting tired he turned back towards the shore. Shilpa was glad that after a lapse of many years she had swam again and in her enthusiasm she had tired herself.

Raj helped her reach the shore and Shilpa on being exhausted lay slumped in the ankle deep water breathing heavily.

As Shilpa lay still regaining her lost energy Raj finally had the chance of ogling over her body. The fair complexion of her skin against the dark swim suit was an awesome sight and his eyes were engrossed on her heaving chest. Her big breasts, most of which not covered in her bikini top had spilled out.

Chapter 5

Looking at the exposed part of her creamy swollen breasts Raj got fired up. He diverted his stare from her bosom to her stomach and looking at the belly button in the centre of the curve of her waist line he felt ecstatic. And when his eyes got glued over her bikini bottom covering her sex he was totally aroused. The impression of the "V" between her legs was breath-taking and the crease where her thighs joined was incredible.

Looking at him staring at her Shilpa crisscrossing her legs smiled at him.

Raj did not object this time but moving closer he placed his hand on her knee and cooing her said "you seem to be tired."

"Yes it has been a long time since I swam" she replied relaxing a bit.

"I hope you have not got any cramps" he asked moving his hand on her knees and parting them.

"No but my legs are little stiff" she replied.

"A massage can soothe them," saying this he caressed her inner thighs.

As he let out the words she looked up at him and seeing his genuine interest in him she said "maybe later."

"Why don't you change the suit, you may catch cold" he said.

This too showed his concern for her and as her eyesight drifted down over his legs she was thrilled to see his pubic hair peeping out of his short briefs. She got so thrilled watching it that her eyes were glued on to the spot.

Raj seeing her showing interest slowly spread his legs which made his pubic hair stuck out of his briefs more prominently and when her gaze shifted to the top of his briefs, she could clearly see the outline of his aroused manhood. This sight aroused her and she could not pull back her sight.

Raj took advantage of it and as Shilpa was staring at his manhood he brought his hand over his upper thighs and by way of scratching it he squeezed his cock for a split second before withdrawing his hand.

Shilpa on seeing him squeeze his cock felt a hot desire swept over her body. She started to writhe in passion and instinctively her hand went over to her bosom and caressed it slowly.

Raj saw the change in her and moving closer he held her hand which was placed on her bosom and said "allow me"

Shilpa looked at him with pent up desire. Her body was aflame and when Raj pushed her hand away and placed his hand on her breast, she took a deep breath which made her breasts to swell and when Raj sliding his fingers inside the swim suit bared them a little and said "most marvelous ones" her body sizzled with passion.

Shilpa moaned on having heard his words and as she looked down at her exposed mounds of flesh she was so ecstatic on seeing her own breasts that she took a deep breath protruding them up.

Raj leaning on her slipped his fingers inside her top and when his hands cupped one full breast in it he dipped his face and pecking a kiss on the warm flesh said "they are so soft and warm."

Shilpa was ecstatic and instinctively her hand went over his head and her fingers started curling his hair.

Raj then started sliding the straps of her swim suit and when one such strap slid down from her shoulder and exposed her dark nipple, he delicately took it inside his mouth.

Shilpa clenched her hands on his head and held a few strands of his hair in her hands as her body went in raptures with hot pleasure invading her body.

Raj having one nipple in his mouth pushed the other strap down and baring the other breast held it in his hand tenderly.

Shilpa could not believe that Raj was playing with her naked breasts. She could not envisage that one of her breast was in his mouth and the other in his hand. This was unthinkable and as she felt her insides churning she held Raj's hand which was holding her breast hard.

Raj took her hand in his and drawing it down over her belly started caressing it and as she enjoyed it, he pushed her hand inside her swim suit. Shilpa feeling her own fingers on her sex let out a scream and before long her fingers could feel the warmth of her sex, her juices started draining out of it. She climaxed.

As desire gave way to shame, Shilpa removed her hand from her sex and when she turned to get up she felt Raj, hugging her from behind and as she tried to wriggle out of his grip he held her captive in his hold and succeeded in wedging his legs between hers.

Shilpa felt his leg slide between hers and imprison her. Being held captive she leaned her body over his till she felt his aroused manhood wedged between her warm buttocks.

Raj started to push his swollen cock between her mounds. As he applied more pressure he felt his cock slip out of his briefs get lodged between the warm mounds of her buttocks. This rejuvenated him.

Shilpa's body was ignited again on feeling his naked cock over her buttocks. Turning her face she kissed him passionately on his cheeks and in the meantime Raj who had intensified his pounding slipped his hand down and as they felt her warm inner thighs he shot his cum screaming her name repeatedly.

Shilpa felt his body shudder and knew he had shot his load and before he could regain his strength she slipped out of his arms and moving behind the boulder shielded her self from him.

Raj who had ejaculated lay exhausted and it took him a few minutes before he could recover and putting on his clothes as he reached the boulder he said "do you need any help"

Hearing him Shilpa screamed "no, don't come, stand where you are" She had shed her swim suit and was standing naked wiping her body with a towel.

"Why can't I come" asked Raj knowing very well her predicament.

"Because I have no clothes on me" shot back Shilpa.

"So what" asked Raj to taunt her?

"I am without clothes did you not hear me" replied Shilpa covering her body as much as the towel could allow knowing very well that he was teasing her.

"I heard you and that is why I want to come" replied back Raj.

"No, please don't" she pleaded stalling for time as she started dressing up quickly.

"I will not come, only on one condition" he replied.

"And what is that" she asked smilingly as she completed dressing.

"The next time we swim, we will swim in the nude" he said.

"No my dear boy, not in the nude" saying this she stepped in front of him fully dressed.

Raj seeing her dressed up, "this is cheating" he said.

"You deserve it my dear boy" she said poking a finger at his stomach.

"Next time I am going to storm in" he answered.

"Only if you get a chance" she said smiling and moving towards the truck.

Raj tamely followed making faces at her and seeing him upset Shilpa said "you better cheer up my boy."

"I am mad at you" he replied frowning at her.

"Have patience my dear boy and remember patience is always rewarding" she said.

Those words brought much relief to him and moving closer to her he said "I adore you."

"A few seconds before you were mad at me" she said looking at him.

"I have changed my mind now" he replied getting in the truck.

"What made you change your mind so fast" she asked.

"I will tell you when we reach home" he replied.

"Thanks for warning me. I will try to stay out of your reach" she said as she stepped into the truck.

"How will do it" he asked sliding closer.

"I will try to be in the company of Priyanka" she replied.

"What when she goes out" he asked her.

"I will go along with her" she replied laughingly as they reached the house.

<h1 style="text-align:center">Chapter 6</h1>

Parking the truck Shilpa hurried to her room to change her dress. Once inside her room as she undressed and looked at her body she was impressed by the fact that it had not lost its appeal. As she was having her bath her thoughts drifted towards Raj and she felt it was not fair on her part to tease him while he was trying to help sort out her daughter's problem.

This made her to think twice and finally decided to comply with his wish of swimming in nude. The more she thought of it the more aroused she was and when she came out of the room wearing a white sari her heart was beating fast.

Raj who was waiting for her was happy to see her dressed up in whites and when his eyes roamed over body he let out a deep moan which made Shilpa lift her eyebrows.

"You look dazzling in that sari" he said approaching her and putting his arms on her waist.

"Do you like this sari" she asked holding one end of it.

"Yes I like both the sari and the woman wearing it" he replied hugging her.

"Priyanka has arrived" she said as she heard her car.

"I heard it. How about a quick kiss" he asked slipping his hands down and clamping the top of her buttocks.

"No not now. Wait till Priyanka goes in for a change" she replied as she felt his hands on her buttocks.

"I wish she had given us a few moments" he replied as his hands squeezed her buttocks before she did move away.

Shilpa looked at him with want in her eyes and when she turned back she saw Priyanka striding in.

Priyanka was glad that she was back home. The whole day her thoughts had wandered over Raj and her mother. She wanted to be close to them and that was the reason why she did not move to her room but stayed put in their company.

This made both Raj and Shilpa eye each other. They wanted to be alone for few moments as both were in an aroused state of mind. Seeing it did not materialize Raj looked up at Shilpa and said "can I have a cup of coffee"

"Yes, I will get it for you" she replied and went into the kitchen.

"Need any help" saying this Raj followed her.

Meanwhile Priyanka had seen that both were nervous and could not reason it out. When Raj got up and followed her mother, switching on the TV and relaxing on the sofa she said "get me a cup too."

Shilpa was a bit nervous when Raj entered the kitchen behind her. Braving herself she went on preparing the coffee. Raj moving behind her placed his hands on her shoulders and nuzzling his face on the nape of her neck said "you smell lovely"

"You are not supposed to come here" spoke Shilpa softly.

"I came to collect what is due to me" he replied sliding his hands down from her shoulders on to her waist and gripping it.

This made her body relax and taking it easy she asked "what do I owe you."

Drawing her close he said "a kiss"

"Priyanka may come in" replied Shilpa as he pulled her to him.

"Turn around" he commanded.

"You are getting mischievous" saying this she turned to face him.

As Shilpa turned, Raj drawing her body said "come closer"

"The coffee is brewing, is it necessary" asked Shilpa shyly as she inched closer to him?

"Yes" saying this he took her in his arms.

Hearing his words and feeling his arms go around and embrace her; Shilpa felt a hot wave rush up her body. Placing her hands on his neck and bringing her face close to his she kissed him on his lips softly and said "happy."

"No not like that, kiss me on my mouth" saying this he opened his lips.

"I don't know how to" she replied playfully.

"Like this" saying it he rammed his lips over hers and sucking them inside he pushed his tongue deep inside her mouth.

Shilpa went limp in his arms. Her body shuddered with delight and when she felt his hand grope her buttocks she stammered and said "Oh no Raaajesh".

"They are so warm Shilpa" he called by her name caressing her rich buttocks with his hand.

Shilpa was bewildered to hear her name "enough Raj, Priyanka is here" she moaned.

"She is busy watching TV, let me" said Raj as his hand dug into the flesh of her buttocks.

As Raj caressed her buttocks Shilpa whose body was on fire suddenly heard the shrill noise of water boiling. Struggling in his arms she said "let me go, the water is boiling."

"No it can wait" saying this Raj continued caressing her warm buttocks and drew her closer as the water kept boiling.

Shilpa who was ecstatic nudged closer to him and embracing him tightly kissed him passionately. The water went on boiling making shrill noise.

Hearing it Priyanka went in and when she saw her mother kissing Raj she was shell shocked and her insides started to churn. She felt heat rush up her body and when she saw Raj's hand caressing her mother's buttocks, her body was ignited. Priyanka stood staring at them in ecstasy.

When the water reached boiling stage, Shilpa slipped out of Raj's arms and when she turned she saw Priyanka slip out from behind the curtain. Raj too had felt Priyanka's presence. He was certain that she had seen them necking and when Shilpa looked at him in bewilderment he said "don't worry its okay"

Filling three cups of coffee when Shilpa and Raj entered the dark sitting room they saw Priyanka cuddled down on the sofa hiding her emotions. Shilpa finding the dark room to her advantage handed Priyanka a cup and sat by her side. Raj followed suit and sat on the other side of her sandwiching her between them.

As they sat drinking coffee watching, TV Priyanka trying to accommodate them slid down from the sofa and sat down on the thick carpet.

This made Raj to move close to Shilpa and putting a hand over her back drew her.

Shilpa very tamely slid across and putting an arm around Raj rested her head on his shoulders.

Raj was aroused as he found both women close to him. Instinctively he drew Shilpa closer and hugged her.

Shilpa finding his masculine hand grip her body nudged closer to him and placing her head on his chest lay cuddled next to him.

Priyanka hearing the sound of their clothes rustling turned her face upwards and looking at them holding each other said "you two seem to be very cozy."

"It is very chill over here" answered Raj winking at her.

"Yes I know it" replied Priyanka turning her attention back to the TV.

As soon as Priyanka turned her face Raj brought his right hand down and hiding it from Priyanka's view placed it over Shilpa's knee.

Shilpa felt his hand on her knee and seeing it well hidden she kept her cool.

It was then Raj kneading her knee slid his hand a little up.

Shilpa squirmed in delight as his hand found her warm thigh.

Seeing her enjoy his move Raj brought his other hand down and holding her face he lifted it up before he kissed her lips softly.

Shilpa was aroused by the soft kiss. She was aroused as Raj had kissed her in the very presence of her daughter. This invigorated her and she complied back by pecking a soft kisses on his lips.

This recharged Raj and he slid his right arm up her thigh and caressed it.

Shilpa moaned softly and continued kissing him lightly. As this provoked Raj he slid his hand further up feeling the warm flesh of her inner thighs while he silently slid his tongue inside Shilpa's mouth.

Shilpa who was in an aroused state opened her mouth and without making any noise started to suck on his tongue.

It made Raj's manhood be fully aroused and the more his hand felt her warm inner thighs the more his engorged manhood pained being imprisoned in his tight pants. The pain was becoming unbearable.

As Shilpa drew her mouth out to take a breath she found Raj's hand which was on her thighs visible to Priyanka if she turned. This made her take his hand and pushed it down till it was hidden behind Priyanka's back.

Raj then pushed his hand further down and holding the bottom of her sari he started to lift it up while with the other he slid under her sari and cupped her breasts.

Shilpa was thrilled when she felt one of his hand cup her breast and the other pulling her sari up. Her body shuddered and warm sensations crept between her thighs. She was on the verge of a climax.

Raj at that very moment felt that she was on the threshold of orgasm and to make it more enjoyable to her, he slipped his hand under her sari and feeling the naked flesh of the back of her legs he caressed it.

Shilpa felt as if she was in an oven. Her body trembled with passion and when Raj's other hand slid inside her blouse and held her breast she felt a stream gush out from her sex. She shivered as unbearable pleasure took over her body.

It was then that Raj looked into her eyes and when she smiled at him he shifted his gaze down at his inflamed manhood which had tented up in his pants. Shilpa followed his stare and when her eyes fell upon his engorged manhood she was mystified. She dropped her eyelids indicating that her daughter was sitting close by and when Raj shook his head she felt aghast.

Raj without bothering Priyanka's presence took hold of her hand and bringing it down he directed it on his manhood.

Shilpa shook her head and when Raj was adamant she placed her hand on his thighs and gripped them hard.

Raj still holding her hand directed it to caress his thighs and when a hesitant Shilpa heeded to it she again felt a hot desire engulf her body. Throwing all caution to the wind she gripped the insides of his thighs, hiding her hand from being seen, and slowly started squeezing them moving her hand upwards.

Raj was excited as Shilpa started to caress his inner thighs. He leaned forward bringing his body in front to hide her actions. His manhood started to pulsate in his pants. Though it pained the pleasure of her caress was unimaginable and when Shilpa's hand proceeded up he dug his hand deeper into her blouse and cupped one full breast in his hand.

Shilpa was thrilled feeling his hand digging deeper in her blouse and instinctively her hand moved up caressing his thighs roughly and when Raj cupped her naked breast in his hand and cupped it she pushed her hand up between his inner thighs till she felt the hot spot of his body.
Raj body shuddered on feeling the delicate touch of her fingers right under his manhood. He widened his thighs to give her room and when Shilpa without hesitating moved her hand over his manhood and stroked it lightly his body convulsed and he shot his cum.

Shilpa felt his manhood jerk underneath her hand and she knew that he had ejaculated. Giving his manhood a final squeeze she pulled out her hand. Both were ecstatic as both had climaxed right in front of Priyanka.

Raj conveyed his thanks with a smile and when Shilpa reciprocated it he kissed her passionately which made Priyanka look back at them.

Both Raj and Shilpa pulled back from kissing each other and when Priyanka said "I am hungry" Shilpa got up and strode into the kitchen.

As Shilpa left the room Raj looked down at Priyanka whose eyes were glistening and sliding down on the carpet he put his hand across Priyanka's back and held her.

Priyanka was glad that at last she had his attention and she snuggled closer to him and asked "how was the kiss"

Raj shied and said "which kiss"

"I saw you kissing my mother" she said blushingly.

"Yes, I kissed your mother. She is a gorgeous woman" he replied back.

"Do you like kissing so much" she asked.

"Yes, I love kissing these lips" he said touching her lips delicately with his fingers.

"Does kissing on the lips excite you so much" she asked.

"Yes it is very exciting to kiss them," saying this he kissed her lips fervently.

Coming out of his hold she asked "whose lips do you like most."

For this he did not have any ready answer. He took a few moments before he said "your lips are captivating, while your mothers are voluptuous ones and both are very stimulating"

So you like both the pairs.

"Yes and it is good fortune that I have kissed both of you" he replied smilingly.

"I saw your hands on her behind, does it also excite you" she asked.

"Oh! Priyanka you are very naïve. Every charm a woman possess is exciting to look, touch and feel" he replied.

"What charms" she asked suddenly.

"Well, your face, your lips, your bosom, your waist, your behind, your thighs are all very exciting to look and feel" he replied.

"Have you seen any of her charms" she asked inquisitively.

Chapter 7

"I had the opportunity to see her breasts" he replied.

"Did you touch them" she asked.

"Yes, I had my hand inside her blouse" he replied.

"And"

"And even caressed her lush thighs a bit" he said.

"Did it excite her as much as it did for you" she asked.

"Obviously" he shot back.

"Did she feel any of you" she asked.

"She placed her hand once on mine" he replied coyly.

"Mine what" she asked?

"My pecker" he replied.

"So you both felt each other's parts" she asked.

"She did not allow me to touch hers" he replied looking down at her waistline.

"Why" she asked suddenly.

"May be she is too shy" he said.

"Oh! Saying this she blushed.

"Why are you blushing" he asked.

"No nothing" she said.

"Tell me" he persisted.

"I thought you had seen her nude body" she said.

"No I did not get the opportunity" he said.

"You know something" she blurted out suddenly.

"What" he asked.

"Yesterday night I was with her" she said.

"And"

"And we bared others upper body" she said.

"You mean you saw each others breasts" he asked.

"Yes" she replied.

"Did it excite you" he asked and waited impatiently for her answer.

"If you call that excitement, yes I was excited" she replied.

"Does talking with me excite you" he asked.

"I am feeling warm sensations" she replied.

"All over your body" he asked.

"Yes all through my body" she replied.

"Any specific place" he asked.

"I can't tell you that" she said shyly.

"Look mine is regaining its strength" he said looking at his pants tenting up.

"What made it to regain its strength" she asked curiously.

"Talking with you about it" he said.

"Can I see it now" she asked.

Raj was excited to hear her words and said "no not now, I need to have a bath."

"Okay, even I too have not taken a bath" saying this she got up and left him.

Raj could not believe the conversation he had with her. Feeling elated he went up to his room and had a leisure bath.

Meanwhile Priyanka after having finished her bath came out wearing a bright sari and Shilpa seeing her decked up said "what's the occasion."

"Nothing just like that" she replied.

"Raj will be happy to see you" she said.

Hearing it she blushed and said "yes I think so, we just had a talk"

"What did you talk about" she asked her.

"Nothing, may be he will tell me more when I go to his room" she replied.

"Yes and I am happy to hear it" she said.

"Can I stay in his room for sometime" she asked.

"Yes" she replied.

On being permitted Priyanka was delighted and she waited impatiently for supper time.

Finding Shilpa alone fixing the dining table Raj moved behind her and held her by placing his hands on her waist.

"What are you doing" asked Shilpa.

"I am trying to warm myself" he replied back.

"Shall I switch on the heater" she asked.

"Your body has more warmth than any heater" he replied as he felt her warm thighs.

"Are you using my body as a heater" she asked.

"No I am using your body for his purpose" he said.

"For whose purpose" she asked bashfully.

"The one which is knocking at your hind" he replied as he moved closer to her so that she could feel his manhood.

"Are you not ashamed" she said.

"Why should I be" he said.

"What happens if my daughter see us" she replied.

"Let her see, moreover I feel she is showing some interest in it" he replied.

"Is she" she asked?

"Yes we just had a talk and she is showing keenness to learn a few things" he said.

"Then why don't you go teach her" she said playfully and waited for his reply.

"I need this as it is cozier" he said as his hands moved up her thighs.

"Do you think I will allow you that liberty" she asked blushingly.

"You have to" he replied back.

"How come" she said as she felt her body sway towards his in passion?

"It is a deal I am going to make with you" he replied.

"What deal" she asked.

"I will teach Priyanka and in return I want to see this" he said as he squarely placed his hand on her mound.

Shilpa shook her head as his hands reached her sex and moving out of his reach said "I am yet to decide on it."

"I know what your decision is" said Raj eyeing her as he sat down on the chair.

"Do you" asked Shilpa as Priyanka came.

After having supper Raj got up from the table and winking at Shilpa went to his room. Priyanka hurrying across the kitchen fetched a glass of milk and looking at her mother, who nodded her head, went up the stairs.

Priyanka hesitated as she approached the door and when she finally entered she felt his muscular arms slip around her waist dragging her in.

Moving inside the room she said "wait till I close the door."

"No Priyanka I have been waiting for this moment from a long time" he replied.

"Don't you want your milk, it is getting spilled" she said.

"Keep it aside. I need something warm" he replied pulling her.

"Shall I switch on the heater" she asked as she set aside the glass of milk.

"Who needs the heater when I have you" he replied turning her to face him.

"Then what do you want" she asked softly.

"I want you in my arms" he said.

"You had me in your arms yesterday" she replied.

"Yesterday you were not the same Priyanka as of today" he said.

"Why? have I changed so much" she asked.

"Yes you have changed a lot. You have grown up. You have become mature" he replied as his eyes wandered over her body.

"Do you see any change in my appearance" she asked as she saw him eyeing her body.

"Yes you look attractive in this sari as it shows off your charms" he said sliding the top of her sari from her chest and looking at her petite bosom ensconced in her blouse.

"What charms are you talking about" she asked getting excited.

"Your breasts they are absolutely ravishing to look at" he said looking at them well settled inside her blouse.

"How can you be so sure when they are covered" she asked as her body sizzled with pleasure.

"I had the pleasure of looking at them yesterday and more over now I can see their cute impressions" he replied as he started releasing the hooks of her blouse one by one.

"Do you think it is necessary to remove my blouse" she asked taking a deep breath.

"Yes I want you to enjoy it thoroughly" he replied removing the blouse from her body.

"Are you doing this for my pleasure" she asked getting elated.

"I take pleasure in pleasuring you" saying this he pulled her blouse from her body and looking at her small breasts set inside her bra said "they are magnificent"

"Don't you think they are small compared to mothers" said Priyanka as her body trembled with desire.

"Yes they are small but they are so beautiful petite and firm" he said as he stared at her breasts under her bra.

"I would like mine to be as big as mother's" she said.

"They will be of her size soon" he replied.

"How soon" she asked.

"Once you get pregnant" he observed.

Hearing it Priyanka was devastated. She had some inkling as to what pregnancy meant and feeling shy she said "I am not going to get pregnant."

"Is it How can you be so sure Do you think my brother will not make you pregnant" he asked.

"Is that the reason why he tries to take advantage of me" she asked.

"What does he do" Raj asked getting excited.

"He is a beast. He usually undresses me in a hurry and pushes his thing inside" she replied shyly.

"Does he not kiss you, fondle your body, undress you slowly and then push his thing inside" he asked.

"No he does not have so much time with him. He does everything in a jiffy" she replied.

"You mean he just . . . . . you, no foreplay" he could not utter the word "fuck"

"Yes he is in and out in a few seconds" she replied.

"And that is why you call him a beast" he asked her.

"Yes and I am scared when he comes to the room during nights" she replied.

"Have you seen his thing" he asked.

"No I have just felt it" she said.

"Does he not undress in front of you" he asked.

"No he just unzips his pants and puts it through" she replied.

"I am so sorry to hear it Priyanka" he said.

"Why are you so" she asked looking puzzled

"Because he does not treat you like a woman" he replied.

"Why do you think he behaves like that" she asked.

"I think there is some deficiency in him" he replied.

"Like," she asked.

"May be he cannot keep his thing vitalized for long" he replied.

"Why is it so" she asked enthusiastically.

"Because you are very pretty and when he sees you naked he just ejaculates or may be his thing is small" he replied.

"May be" she said dejected.

"You don't have to feel sorry about it. Speak to him to consult a doctor" he replied.

"No I cant do that. What will he think about me" she replied flatly.

"You have to do it for your sake" he replied.

"Is it necessary" she asked him quizzically.

"Yes it would be to your advantage" he said.

"Why don't you speak to him" she asked him suddenly.

"No I cant, those matters can only be discussed between a husband and a wife" he said.

"But you are talking to me and you are not my h. . . . . " she stopped.

"Yes, I am talking to you about it coz I was told to do so" he said.

"By whom" she asked.

"By your mother and maybe your husband asked her to do so" he replied.

"Yes, he had addressed a letter to her which I handed over" she replied.

"Yes, may be that is the reason why your mother asked for my help" he said.

"So you are helping me out. What is there for you" she asked him.

"There is plenty in it for me" he replied back.

"And that is" she asked.

"That is I have pretty Priyanka and her gorgeous mother for company" he said.

"Are you happy with it" she asked.

"Of course, I could not have dreamt of anything more" he replied.

"You are trying to teach me that I can understand. What about my mother" she asked?

"Remember she is a lonely woman after losing her husband.
She too needs some male company" he said.

"How nice of you to help us both" she said.

"It is my pleasure" he replied smiling broadly.

"Now that you have taught me everything shall I go" she asked trying to button up her blouse.

"No what I taught you was theory but the practical remains" he said.

"Why don't you go to mother for the practical" she said shyly.

"She does not need any lessons. It is you who are in need of it" saying this he pulled her to him.

"No I don't need it, I have learnt a lot already" she replied naughtily as he pulled her to him.

"Tell me what you have learnt" he asked engulfing her in his arms.

"That you are a crazy guy who needs two women to get satisfied" she replied.

"Yes very true" saying this he pushed her on the bed.

Priyanka was stunned when he pushed her on the bed and on regaining her senses, as she looked up she saw him removing his shirt and pants.

"What is that for" she asked as his well masculine chest was bared.

"To be comfortable while teaching you" he replied.

"Comfortable in teaching me what" she asked as waves of heat surged through her body and on seeing him drop his pants exposing his erect maleness hidden behind his shorts.

"To teach you how to make love" he replied as he bent down and took hold of her hands.

"Teach me" she replied as he lifted and placed her evenly on the bed.

"Yes, let me remove this out first" saying it he took hold of her sari and deftly removed it off her body.

Priyanka was pleased with his casualness. She saw that he was not showing any kind of urgency like her husband and motivated by it she said "you are so nice"

"And you are so pretty" saying this his hands roamed over her waist searching for the cord holding her slip and on loosening it and sliding it down her legs he said "your body is so beautifully carved"

"Why does my husband not speak of it" she wondered as she felt her slip been drawn out of her body. Priyanka lay still clutching the bedspread with her hand lying there with only her bra and panties. She was totally aroused by his staring.

Raj after discarding her slip stay put gazing at her exquisite body which was so slender and so perfect. He saw the lithe body of Priyanka lying motionless there to be taken. At one stage he felt a strong urge to rip apart her panties and raid her but soon changed his mind seeing her delicate features.

His eyes took to her slender waist curved in and her belly button which was almost invisible lodged at the centre of her stomach. His eyes took to her rib cage and the small upheavals of her breasts. Her long neckline added to her charm and as he looked down he could not make out any impressions of her sex as it was well covered by the dark color of her panties.

Her long sleek legs wriggling with pleasure was a sight to behold and when he took his time looking at her body, Priyanka suddenly thrust her hands up and pulled Raj down.

As Priyanka pulled him Raj could not control himself any longer. Lying flat over her he took her face in his hands and said "I feel as if I am dreaming."

"No you are not dreaming this is happening" she said blushingly.

"Priyanka you look so different" he said as he covered her lower body with his and cupped her face in his hand.

"Is it to your advantage" she asked feeling his eyes penetrate hers deeply which was just a shade away from hers. His lips quivering, his tongue was moving in circles wetting them.

"Yes, only if you would allow me to kiss these soft lips" he said as his fingers touched them.

"Who's stopping you, kiss me Raj" she spoke softly.

"No let me first fulfill my desire of embedding this lovely face in my mind" he said.

"Why, have you not seen me earlier" she asked.

"No, not when you were looking so ravishing" he replied.

"Oh Raj" she screamed before she locked her lips over his and kissed him hard. Raj was delighted and opening his mouth wide he took her lips inside and started lapping them with his tongue.

Priyanka was electrified on finding her lips engulfed in his mouth. Putting her arms around his back she drew his head only to find him sucking more of her lips into his mouth.

Having imprisoned her lips in his mouth Raj hands flew at her back and in one simple notion unhooked her bra and slid it out from her body.

Priyanka on having her bra discarded lifted her body upwards squashing her petite breasts on his masculine chest and embraced him.

Raj felt her small hard erect nipples poke at his chest as Priyanka embraced. Not withstanding the pleasure aroused from it and craving to take a look at her naked breasts he drifted down releasing Priyanka lips from his.

What he saw of her breasts made his mouth dribble saliva. Priyanka's small firm rounded breasts were a delight to see. Her dark teats embedded in the middle of her creamy flesh were a sight to behold. He brought his hand down and with the tip of his finger he started circling the roughness around her teats.

This made Priyanka squirm her body in ecstasy. Her body trembled with pleasure unknown to her. She tried to thrash her legs which were pinned down by his. The muscles in her cunt began to quiver and when Raj brought his face down and took her nipple inside his mouth her dam burst opened and she came. She climaxed. Her body convulsed. She whipped her arms around the bed holding whatever came in contact with it.

Raj was pleased to have her climaxed. Though he had enjoyed it he had taken care to see that she derived the maximum pleasure out of it. It was a few moments later that Priyanka stopped thrashing her body and cooled down and when she opened her eyes he saw that they were the eyes of a satisfied woman.

Priyanka opened her eyes and looked at him with moist eyes which spoke of her fond love to him. She thanked him profusely and when Raj nodded his head accepting it Priyanka kissed him lightly on his lips.

"Did you enjoy it" asked Raj when she pulled her lips out.

"It was the best time I ever had and I don't know how to repay you back" she said.

"It is quite simple" replied Raj.

"And what is that" she asked him more daringly.

"Reveal to me what my eyes are so impatient to see" he said.

"What is there that can satisfy your eyes" she said sliding up on the bed.

"What everyman craves to look? The most valued treasure a woman possesses" he said.

"I don't have any treasure which either I cannot show or share with you" she replied.

"Then pull down your panties and reveal it to me" he said.

"Is that what you are so eager to see? Will revealing it satisfy you" she fired the question back to him.

"Yes to be frank with you, my eyes have never had the opportunity to see any" he replied.

"Is it a fact? Is this the first time you are going to see it" she asked him.

"Yes, you would be the first women to reveal it" he replied.

"You are at a liberty to see anything" she said moving further up on the bed.

"Can you not pull it down for me" he said looking at the patch of cloth covering her sex.

"My, my" saying this Priyanka slid her delicate fingers inside her panties and holding the waist band started rolling it down.

Raj's eyes popped up when the fabric started sliding down revealing the patch of her dark pubic hair and when she was through with the process of sliding it out of her body, he for the first time saw the pinkish slit of her cunt hidden behind a veil of thin black hair which instantly made his prick throbbing. "It's magnificent" he cried out.

"Is it really so" asked Priyanka.

"Yes Priyanka it is truly magnificent and thank you so much for revealing it" he said as his fingers cleared the pubic hair and stared deeply at her pulsating cunt.

"Well now that you have seen it" she said shyly.

Raj could not get the meaning of it and when he lifted his head and saw her blushing red face it suddenly struck him. "Do you want to see" he asked.

Priyanka bowed her head shyly.

Lifting himself Raj moved over and taking hold of her soft hand he guided it to his cock and said "it is yours."

Priyanka was elated when her hand felt the hardness of his cock over his shorts and as Raj waited she delicately held it.

Raj's body went into raptures when he felt her fingers take hold of his cock. Pushing her hand inside his shorts he made her take possession of his naked cock.

Priyanka's delicate fingers circled his hot hard naked cock and her desires shot up. Instinctively she pushed his shorts down with the other and looking at what she had bared her body started to writhe in passion.

Priyanka was so pulverized on looking at the thick hard erect cock that her legs went limp. Her eyes took to its shaft which she felt was more than eight inches long and she had difficulty circling her fingers around it.

Raj saw her looking curiously at it and when he said do you like it, "it is huge," she replied.

Raj laughed at her words and said "it would be perfect for you."

"What" said Priyanka and looked up at him.

"I said it would fit you perfectly" replied back Raj.

"No Raj I feel it would not ... ... " she said.

"Why" asked Raj drawing her closer?

"Don't you think it is big" she said still holding his cock in her hand.

"Yes it is big and you would love it more" he replied.

"I think I can't take it in" she said.

"You can, just lie down and relax" he said as he tenderly pushed her down on the bed.

"Are you sure you are going to put it in" she asked as her body sizzled in anticipation.

"Yes, I am going to put it in" saying this he crawled between her thighs and going on his knees he positioned his cock above her cunt.

"Oh Raj" she cried as she felt the tip of his cock at the opening of her cunt.

"Relax dear, relax" saying this he grooved his cock till its head poked inside her hot opening.

"You are hurting me" cried Priyanka as she put her arms around him and hugged him.

Chapter 8

"Did it not hurt you when your husband did it" he asked.

"His is not as big as yours" she replied.

"Does it hurt now" he said as he gave a light push till his cock head penetrated inside.

"Not much" said Priyanka as she felt her cunt accommodating his cock in.

"Now' he said as he gave a further push enabling his cock to slide two inches inside her cunt.

"Has it gone in completely" she asked biting her lips and getting thrilled by having accommodated it.

"I am almost there" he said giving a final push.

"Oh my, you are in" she cried as she felt his cock head ramming the delicate walls of her cunt.

"Yes Priyanka, it is in" he said as he pushed it to the hilt.

"Raj" screamed Priyanka as she felt the rock hard cock ramming inside her cunt and as he started thrusting it deeper the pain gave to pleasure and Priyanka lifting her head searched for his lips and on finding them said "fuck me."

Raj was thrilled to hear those and it suddenly made me pound her delicate cunt with fervor.

Priyanka sucking his lips reciprocated his moves and soon she felt the same sensations creeping inside her body. She knew she was going to cream again and when Raj started pounding the insides of her cunt she bit his lips and doused her cunt with her juices.

Raj felt her cunt pulsating and as this added to his vigor he started to ram his cock inside her cunt furiously till he felt his cock started vibrating and when he was on the verge of shooting he removed his cock and let his cum spray over her body.

Priyanka was shocked to see him spurt the thick fluid on her waist. This was the first time she had seen a cock shooting cum and curiously she brought her hand down and felt the thick semen. Feeling the thick warm liquid in her hand she suddenly had the desire to taste it and when she saw Raj lying by her side exhausted she slipped her fingers inside her mouth and tasted the salty cum. She was delighted to have done it.

Raj lying by her side saw her licking her fingers. This invigorated him and turning to face her said "do you like its taste"

"Yes, it tastes good" she replied coyly.

"Want more" he asked.

"What" she asked puzzled as she had thought he had drained every drop.

"There is plenty from where it came" he said.

Priyanka looked at him and could not stop herself from asking "are you sure."

"Yes, I have plenty, take me in your mouth" he said.

"You mean you want that inside my mouth" she asked.

"Yes, I want him in your mouth" he replied looking at his cock which was regaining its strength.

"How can I take such a big one" she asked.

"The same way as your cunt did" he replied getting up and positioning himself over her face.

"It is very big" she said holding his shaft in her hand.

"You can take it and moreover you will love it having it inside your mouth" he said.

When Priyanka heard his words she suddenly felt curious to try it. Holding his cock in her hand she was thrilled to regain its full size. Her fingers went bracing over the veined cock and the more she held it the more she liked it.

Raj seeing her fondling his cock brought his hand down on her face and pushed his fingers inside her mouth.

Priyanka opened her mouth to accommodate his fingers.

Raj curving his fingers inside her hot mouth widened her lips and as she was enjoying his ministrations he slid his cock head down until it was lodged at the opening of her mouth.

Priyanka was surprised on having his cock head in her mouth which made her body ignite again. She held his cock hard in her hand and when Raj removed his fingers and gave a push.

Priyanka released her hold and the huge cock slowly drifted into her mouth. At first she felt uneasy to have his cock inside her mouth but when she felt its hot head ramming at the delicate wall of her mouth she started loving it. She maneuvered her tongue around its head and started licking it.

Raj was on cloud nine having thrust his cock fully inside her mouth and when Priyanka started licking it he turned around and moving on top of he brought his face between her slender thighs and started kissing them profusely.

Priyanka let out a moan on feeling his mouth licking her inner thighs. This made her suck his cock eagerly and when she left Raj's lips nearing her cunt she tightened the hold on his cock by closing her lips over it.

Raj felt his cock embed fully inside the hot cavern of her mouth and looking down at the pink opening of her cunt lips staring at him to be invaded; he slipped his tongue deep inside the pulsating cunt.

Priyanka's body shuddered as she felt his tongue snake inside her hot cunt. Instinctively she closed her cunt lips over it and entrapped it.

Raj pushed his tongue deep inside till it felt her clitoris. Priyanka reciprocated by sucking his cock as waves of hot pleasure started running up her body.

Raj nuzzled his face deeper and taking her cunt lips in his he started sucking them vigorously as he felt she was nearing an orgasm.

Priyanka could not sustain it any longer and thrashing her legs she creamed again.

Raj continued sucking her cunt till her spasms subsided and when he saw her cool down he started penetrating his cock deeper into her mouth.

Priyanka felt his cock reach the hilt and lifting herself up she allowed him more access.

Raj on feeling her elevate her body started ramming his cock inside and Priyanka feeling his deep thrusts held his cock in her hand and when his thrusts got magnified she started pulling his cock in and out of her mouth. This made Raj's body to tremble and soon his cock started pulsating. Giving one final push he started shooting deep inside her throat.

Priyanka felt his cock spraying inside her mouth which made her want to look at it and the moment she withdrew it out she saw it spray her face with his cum which was a sight to behold.

Raj was exhausted on emptying his balls and when Priyanka pulled out his cock from her mouth he took her in his arms and hugged her taking whatever comforts her body could give.

Priyanka was elated with the happenings of the night and when she saw Raj exhausted she got up and finding her clothes went out of his room.

As she was about to enter her room she suddenly felt a desire to talk to her mother and when she entered her mother's room and saw her lying with her body partially uncovered. On seeing her heaving breasts and legs partially bare a desire shot through her body and on impulse her hand started caressing her own breasts.

Shilpa who was awake had waited impatiently for Priyanka to come. She was anxious to know what had happened but when she saw in the dim light Priyanka standing near her and fondling her own breasts a want shot through her and lifting her hand she entwined her fingers with her daughters.

Priyanka kept her fingers entangled with her mothers while with the other continued caressing her breasts and Shilpa seeing her daughter in an aroused state lifted her hand up and slowly tugged her sari down exposing her blouse which was loosely held by the hooks.

Priyanka removed her hand from her breasts as she let her mother's fingers finish the act of removing the blouse from her body.

Shilpa after drawing out her blouse brought her hand over her breasts caressed them softly over her bra.

Priyanka stood shivering with excitement and when her mother's hands which were caressing her breasts reached down on her waist and started pulling out her sari she moved closer to the cot allowing her hands more access.

Shilpa after removing Priyanka's sari pulled the cord of her slip and when she slid it down her legs she placed both her hands on her firm buttocks and pulled her lightly towards her.

Priyanka moved closer to her mother. Her mother's face was just inches from her scorching cunt and she felt her mother's eyes prying deeply.

Shilpa gripped her daughter's buttocks firmly in one hand and with the other she started pulling down her panties.

This made Priyanka's body to tremble and before she could react she felt her mother's face on her hot opening. She screamed Mama as Shilpa kissed her daughter's cunt and poked her tongue in it.

Priyanka climaxed as her mother sucked her cunt and as she regained her senses she climbed on the bed and squatting by her side started to undressed her mother. Shilpa helped her daughter in discarding her dress and when she was totally nude she pulled her daughter's face close to her cunt and said "yes, kiss Mama there."

Thus they lay kissing each other and it was quite late in the morning when Shilpa got up and went into the kitchen.

Raj waited for Priyanka or Shilpa to come to his room and as none of them appeared, he got up and after having a wash strolled down the steps to see Shilpa brewing coffee in the kitchen.

Shilpa heard him come down the steps. Switching off the gas as she turned to look at him she saw a totally different Raj. He was walking tall with an air of authority in him. He face was gleaming; he was walking as if he had conquered the world. He was sporting a huge smile and on entering the kitchen he came near her and stood by her side.

Shilpa braved herself and turning her face welcomed him with a smile.

Moving close by, he said "can I have some coffee"

"Sure" saying this as Shilpa turned she felt him placed his hands on the sides of her buttocks with authority. She was in a dilemma as she could not stop his moves. Today was a different day and she knew she was on the back foot. As his hand slid down over her buttocks a desire started building up her body. Standing still she let his hands take control of her body.

Raj on seeing that she did not object slowly started to caress her buttocks. This made Shilpa to wriggle her body with pleasure and as his hand slid between the cracks of her buttocks she let out a deep moan.

Though Shilpa enjoyed his ministrations she was worried as Priyanka was at home.
Many a times she turned back to see whether she was up and then looked at him.

Raj saw her turning around and read the message she wanted to convey. He was not bothered whether Priyanka would see them or not. He was in a mood to arouse her deeply and he carried out by pushing the palm of his hand deep between the cracks of her buttocks.

This made Shilpa to cry out in ecstasy and hesitating a little she pushed back till his hand was well lodged between her warm buttocks.

Raj to tease her withdrew his hand when he felt Shilpa squirm in pleasure and looked over her shoulders as if nothing had happened.

Shilpa resigned as he withdrew his hands and filling a cup of coffee he handed it to him.

Raj took the coffee from her and when Shilpa turned back he again slipped his hand, this time on the back of her inner thighs and pushed it between them.

Shilpa bit her lips hard. She did not let out a moan as she depressed it thinking he could pull back his hand.

Raj pushed his hand deeper. He could feel the heat generating from her body elope on to his hand. He felt his cock which had risen straining in his pants; he slid his hand further up her thighs.

Shilpa felt his hand amidst her sari bracing up and the more he thrust it in she knew he was close to her cunt. This made her cunt quiver with excitement. Her body went limp which made her lean on him.

Raj was delighted to have her lean her body upon his. Bringing one hand on her waist and pulling her body on to his aroused cock and sliding the other up her thighs said "you are very hot there"

Shilpa was aghast to hear his words and his hand nuzzling over her cunt. She squirmed in delight and said "so you have finally captured it."

"Yes, it was a pleasure reaching it" he replied.

"I know what other pleasure you had yesterday night" she said.

"Did she tell you about it" he asked bracing his lips on her shoulders.

"Yes everything that happened yesterday night" she replied.

"She told me what you did to her" Raj replied.

"What did I do to her" she asked nervously.

"You took her in your arms and sucked her breasts" he replied.

"I did that as I had to soothe her" Shilpa replied.

"And I did it as you wanted me to teach her" he replied.

"And enjoyed it up to the hilt" she asked.

"No not up to the hilt" he shot back.

"Why not" she asked and turned to face to him.

"I have yet to conquer this" he said as he pushed his hand up and cupped her warm cunt.

"Oh! Raj are you not content with what you had yesterday" she asked.

"No I am only half way through and moreover you promised" he said.

"What did I promise" she asked.

"That we will go swimming in nude" he replied.

"So you want to see my nude body" she asked.

"No I have changed my mind now. We are not going to swim in nude" he replied.

As these words puzzled Shilpa, "then what" she asked.

"Take me to the secluded spot in your vine yard" he replied.

"Why" asked Shilpa getting excited by the very thought of it.

"I will tell you there" he replied.

"Very cunning" she replied disengaging from him as she heard Priyanka enter the room.

Priyanka strolled into kitchen and as it was late for her she grabbed a few sandwiches and left.

As Priyanka left a maid arrived for her weekly chores. This made both Raj and Shilpa draw into a shell and after having their breakfast they went to their respective rooms to change.

Shilpa arrived decked in a smart cotton sari. She had let her hair loose and had tied her sari just below her navel revealing much of her vast bulging waist to his gaze and as she stepped into the truck Raj had a fleeting glance of her legs which made him aroused.

It was sometime before they reached the vine yard and Shilpa went deep into the woods before she stopped on the other side of the lake. The spot had lush green grass and cool breeze was blowing from the lake.

Getting down from the truck they strolled down till they came between thick foliage where Shilpa braving herself and taking a deep breath said "well, do you like this spot."

"Yes, it is close to the one I had in mind" saying it he sat on the green grass resting his back on the trunk of a tree.

"Shall I get a sheet" asked Sheet seeing him sitting on the grass.

"Not necessary" saying this he pulled her down.

This time Shilpa did not hesitate. As he pulled her down she lay beside him placing her head on his shoulders and said "thanks."

"Why are you thanking me" he asked.

"For everything you did to us" she replied.

"It was my pleasure and you know it very well" he said.

"But still you were so kind, so patient and so very understanding" she said.

"Yes you have tested my patience enough" he said as he drew her warm body.

She shied and said "how did I test your patience."

"You made me count minutes before I could have you" he replied.

"When did you have me? In your dreams" she asked smilingly.

"I had you when you agreed for the swim" he replied.

"Were you so sure of it" she asked moving closer.

"Yes when you agreed to wear the two piece swim suit, I was certain" he said.

"Many women wear two piece swim suits" she said.

"Not that which reveals most of their breasts and their pubic hair" he replied.

"Did it" she asked mildly shocked.

"Yes, I had the pleasure of seeing it" he said.

"You are a shameless creature" she said.

"Yes I am a shameless creature" he replied as he started drawing her sari out.

"No Raj not here" she protested feebly.

"Why who is here to see" he replied as he pulled her sari out.

"I feel ashamed" she said.

"What is there to feel ashamed off" he asked.

"You are undressing me under the open sky" she replied and looked up.

"Yes and it gives me more pleasure than being indoors'" he replied as his hands slid on her back.

"You are too much" she said as she resigned.

"You know something" he said as he unhooked her blouse and pulled it out.

"What" hissed Shilpa feeling the blouse slip out of her body?

"Priyanka wants her breasts to be like yours" he said.

"Meaning" she asked.

"She wants them to be full like yours" he said cupping them.

"What about you, do you like them" she asked.

"Let me bare them, then I will speak" saying it he unhooked her bra.

Shilpa was elated when he unhooked her bra and as his eyes wandered over her naked breasts she said "what's your opinion now."

"They are marvelous, gorgeous, and just right enough to cup and play with" saying this he fondled her breasts.

"Raj you are making me dizzy with your words" said Shilpa.

"You possess such a fine pair of breasts" he replied as he started tweaking her nipples.

"When is this going to end Raj" said Shilpa seeing him take his own time fondling and playing with her breasts.

"I wish the time would stand still and allow me to do this for ever" he said.

"Have you not planned to go back" she said lifting her face and kissing him.

"That is the irony. I have to leave soon" he replied as he slipped his hand down on her waist.

"Stay back" spoke Shilpa in his ears.

"I only wish I could" he said as his hand slid inside her petticoat.

"What is your hand doing there" asked Shilpa as her pleasure heightened on finding his hand slip inside her petticoat.

"It is craving to touch and feel what you have not allowed so far" he said.

"But in the morning you felt it" she said.

"Yes, but then you had it covered with your sari, petticoat and what not" he said.

"What else did I wear" she asked suddenly getting hornier.

"You had your panties on and I felt they were damp" he said as his hand slid above her panties and felt her moist sex.

"No you are lying, it was not wet in the morning" she said nibbling his ears.

"But now you are on the verge of wetting it out, is it not" he asked.

"Yes, how do you know it" she asked lifting her body and hugging his.

"I can feel your hot cunt pulsating" he said pressing his fingers between the gaps of her cunt lips.

Hearing him utter the word cunt and feeling his fingers poking in "yes, since morning I am on the verge of coming," as she said this wild convulsions shook her body and moistness leaked out of her cunt soaking her panties.

Raj felt Shilpa's body shook with wild orgasm and he held her trembling body tightly in his grasp. At last when he felt her body relax after the convulsions, "hold mine Shilpa" he said softly.

Shilpa was thrilled on hearing his words. She was thrilled because he had called her by her name and asked her to hold his cock. She hugged him tightly and bringing her lips near his lips "you want me to hold your cock" she said before kissing him passionately on his lips.

Raj was ecstatic when she uttered the word cock. Holding her hand in his he guided it on his swollen cock and placing it over he said "yes Shilpa remove my pants and take my cock."

"My dear boy, my dear boy" saying this Shilpa squeezed his cock over his pants and moving up she straightened in front of him and still holding his erect cock in her hand over his pants said "this seems huge."

Raj was excited. He widened his thighs and looking at Shilpa's hand holding onto his cock said "release him and have a look."

"He is huge Raj" saying this Shilpa unhooked his pants and drawing the zip down she pulled his pants out from his body.

Raj was charged up when he saw Shilpa pull out his pants. Pushing his erect cock in front he said "Priyanka had also the same words to say."

"Poor little Priyanka, she had to endure such a huge one" saying this as she pulled out his briefs, her eyes got transfixed to its swollen head glistening in the day light and looking at it said "Raj you possess a glorious cock."

"It may not be as glorious as the one which you have kept still hidden" he replied looking down at the "V" between her thighs.

Chapter 9

"No Raj this is more wonderful than the one which you want to see so badly" saying this she took hold of his cock in her hand and looking at the blue veins over its shaft she sent her fingers over it till they reached his heavy set of balls.

"If it is not so, then why are you hiding it still" he asked as his hand moved over the object his eyes were hovering on.

"I am hiding it, fearing this huge cock" she replied.

"Why, don't you want it to invade your cunt" he spoke softly as he put his hand over her panties.

"No Raj I am nervous, it may rip me apart" she said as she held his enormous cock in both her hands.

"When your daughter can take it, it would be no problem for you" he said as he placed his hands on her cunt before pushing her panties down.

"It's been a long time" she thought to herself and seeing him about to pull her panties down said "how can you be so sure when you have not seen it" as her body started getting aroused again on his ministrations.

"Because I think your cunt is livelier than your daughters" he said as he slipped her panties down.

Seeing him comparing it to her daughters heightened her pleasure "are you so sure" she asked again as she widened her legs allowing his gaze on her naked cunt.

"Yes, I am positive now. It is the most magnificent" he said as his eyes finally got glued on her exposed cunt hidden amidst the silken black pubic hair and as he spread them carefully, he saw the pinkish lips of her so well carved cunt. He was spellbound on viewing her naked cunt and repeated "this is fully developed, more glorious, and more magnificent than Priyanka's."

Seeing him admiring her cunt Shilpa got aroused and said "are your eyes pleased now. Was this what you wanted to see? Are you satisfied my dear boy."

"Yes Shilpa this is what my eyes always dreamt of seeing" saying this he slowly put her down on the green grass.

"Now what" asked Shilpa seeing him hover up on her?

"Now it is time for the inevitable," saying this he positioned his cock above her cunt.

"What inevitable? Are you eyes not satisfied" Shilpa asked getting excited by his act of getting ready to fuck her.

"Yes my eyes are satisfied but my cock is raging to invade your cunt" he replied.

"You mean you want to fuck me, screw me" she said letting her tongue to go wild, widening her legs and curving her body up to accommodate him.

"Yes Shilpa I am going to fuck you. I am going to fuck Priyanka's mother" saying this he thrust his hot erect cock into the steaming cunt of Shilpa.

Shilpa cried out in ecstasy as she felt his erect cock disappear inside her cunt and holding Raj tightly in her arms said "yes Raj you can fuck me and also fuck my daughter."

Raj started pounding his cock in her cunt, jabbing at the delicate walls of her inner labia and Shilpa on having a male organ ravishing her pulsating cunt after a long long time thrashed her body till she erupted for the second time.

Raj went wild with passion. His cock had invaded Shilpa's cunt right up to hilt and on feeling the edge of her hot wet cunt his cock started shooting his cum right at the bottom of her cum. As his cock shot out he felt exhausted and fell over Shilpa.

Shilpa took him in her arms and held him to her bosom tightly thinking she had only a couple of days to cuddle him as she was sure that he would soon leave her.

END.